The Changeling

by Selma Lagerlöf

Illustrated by Jeanette Winter

*Translated from the Swedish
by Susanna Stevens*

ALFRED A. KNOPF NEW YORK

THIS IS A BORZOI BOOK PUBLISHED BY ALFRED A. KNOPF, INC.

Translation copyright © 1989 by Susanna Marie Farrell Stevens
Illustrations copyright © 1992 by Jeanette Winter

All rights reserved under International and Pan-American Copyright Conventions. Published in the United States by
Alfred A. Knopf, Inc., New York, and simultaneously in Canada by Random House of Canada Limited, Toronto. Distributed by
Random House, Inc., New York. Book design by Edward Miller.

Library of Congress Cataloging-in-Publication Data
Lagerlöf, Selma, 1858-1940. [Bortbytingen. English] The changeling / by Selma Lagerlöf ; translated from the Swedish by
Susanna Stevens ; illustrated by Jeanette Winter.   p.   cm. Translation of: Bortbytingen. Summary: A farmer's wife becomes
the foster mother of a troll's child and her humanistic treatment of the changeling eventually secures the return of her own
son. ISBN 0-679-81035-8 (trade)—ISBN 0-679-91035-2 (lib. bdg.) [1. Trolls—Fiction. 2. Fairy tales.] I. Winter, Jeanette, ill. II.
Title. PZ8.L136Ch   1992 [Fic]—dc20 90-45277

Manufactured in Singapore   10 9 8 7 6 5 4 3 2 1

The Changeling

Once upon a time an old troll woman was walking through the forest with her baby in a birch-bark basket on her back. The baby troll was big and ugly, with bristle-like hair, teeth as sharp as nails, and a claw on its little finger. But the troll mother thought it was the most beautiful baby in the world.

After a time she came to a clearing in the forest. A pathway, rutted and slippery with tree roots, ran through the clearing, and along it a farmer and his wife were riding on horseback.

The moment the troll crone caught sight of them, she wanted to sneak back into the forest so that these human beings would not see her, but when she noticed that the farmer's wife was carrying a baby in her arms, she changed her mind.

"I must see if a human baby can be as beautiful as my own," she thought, and she hid behind a big hazel bush that grew by the pathway.

But when they rode past her, the troll, in her eagerness to see the baby, stretched so far forward that she startled the horses. The farmer and his wife cried out in terror and were nearly thrown from their saddles as the horses reared up and bolted away.

The troll crone whined in anger, for time had permitted her only a glance at the human baby. But then she was happy. For on the ground, at her feet, lay the baby, screaming in fright.

It had been thrown from its mother's arms when the horses reared up, and had landed, unhurt, in a pile of dry leaves. When the troll crone leaned over it, the baby suddenly stopped crying and laughed, reaching out its hands to tug on her black beard.

Bewildered, the troll crone stared at the human baby. She looked at its thin fingers with their pink nails, its clear blue eyes, and its tiny red mouth. She felt its soft hair, stroked its cheek with her hand, and grew more and more amazed. She could not understand how a baby could be so rosy and soft and delicate.

Suddenly, the troll crone pulled the birch-bark basket off her back, removed her own infant, and placed it beside the human baby. And when she saw the difference between them, she began to howl.

Meanwhile, the farmer and his wife had regained control of their horses, and they now turned back to search for their child.

The troll crone could hear them coming, but as she had not yet seen her fill of the human baby, she remained sitting beside it until they were nearly in view.

She then made a decision. Leaving her own infant lying alongside the path, she put the human baby into her basket, tossed it over her shoulder, and scurried into the woods.

She had barely disappeared before the riders reached the clearing. They were handsome countryfolk, the owners of a large farm in the fertile valley below the mountain.

The farmer's wife rode ahead of her husband and was first to catch sight of the baby. She should have understood what kind of baby it was from its frightful shrieking, but she had been so afraid that her little one had been killed in the fall that all she could think was, "Thank God, he is alive!"

"Here is our baby!" she called to her husband, and she slid down from her saddle and hurried over to the troll child.

When the farmer rode up, his wife was inspecting the baby.

"But my baby doesn't have teeth like nails," she said as she turned the baby over and over. "My baby doesn't have hair like boar bristles," she complained, her voice rising in fear. "My baby doesn't have a claw on his little finger!"

The farmer thought that his wife had gone mad, and jumped quickly off his horse.

"Look at this baby, and tell me why he looks so strange!" said the farmer's wife, handing the baby to her husband. He had barely glanced at the baby before he spat three times and flung him down.

"What on earth are you doing?" his wife exclaimed.

"It's a troll child!" he cried out. "It's not our baby." The farmer's wife remained sitting. She could not understand what had happened.

"Don't you see that this is a changeling?" her husband shouted at her. "The trolls were ready and waiting when our horses reared up. They stole our baby and left one of their own in his place."

"Then where's our baby?" asked his wife.

"The trolls took him," said her husband.

The farmer's wife now understood their misfortune. She turned deathly pale, and her husband thought she might die right then and there.

"Our child cannot be far away," he said, attempting to comfort her. "We should search through the forest."

So he tied up the horses and set off into the thicket. His wife stood up and intended to follow him, but then she noticed that the troll child lay where he could easily be kicked by the horses, which were jittery from being so close to him.

Though she shuddered at the mere thought of touching the changeling again, she picked him up and moved him some distance away, to a place where the horses could not reach him.

"Here's the rattle our boy was holding when you dropped him!" shouted the farmer.

The farmer's wife hurried after him, and they walked deep into the forest. But they found neither their child nor the troll crone, and when twilight set in, they were forced to return to their horses.

The farmer's wife cried and wrung her hands. Her husband clenched his teeth and said not a word of comfort. He was angry with his wife for allowing the child to fall. "The child should have been held tight, no matter what," he thought. But when he saw how miserable she was, he had not the heart to reproach her.

He had already helped his wife mount her horse when she remembered the changeling. "What shall we do with the troll child?" she asked.

"Well, where is he?" asked her husband.

"He's over there, under that bush."

"That's a good place for him," said her husband, laughing bitterly.

"Oh, but we can't just leave him here in the wilderness."

"Oh, yes indeed, we can," said the farmer, putting his foot in the stirrup.

The farmer's wife thought that maybe her husband was right. They did not need to take care of the troll's baby. She let her horse take a few steps. But she could not go on. "He's a child, all the same," she said. "I can't leave him here to become food for the wolves."

"He's fine just where he is," her husband replied.

"If you don't hand him to me now, I'll have to come back here for him tonight," said the farmer's wife.

"It's not enough that the trolls have stolen my child. They have obviously turned my wife's head as well," muttered the farmer.

Still, he handed the child up to his wife, for he loved her dearly.

By the next day, the entire parish knew of their misfortune, and all who were learned and wise came to offer advice.

"She who has a changeling in her house must beat him with a heavy cane," said an old woman.

"Why should he be treated so cruelly?" asked the farmer's wife. "He may be ugly, but he's done nothing wrong."

"No, but if you cane the troll child till you draw blood, the troll crone will come rushing back with your child and grab her own. I know of many who've recovered their young ones like that."

"Yes, but those children were no longer alive," added another old woman, and the farmer's wife knew that she could never beat an innocent child.

Later, when she and the changeling were alone in the cottage, she began longing so intensely for her own child that she did not know what she should do.

"Perhaps I should do as I was advised, after all," she thought, but she could not bring herself to do it.

At that very moment the farmer entered the cottage. He held a cane in his hand and asked for the changeling. His wife realized that he intended to follow the old woman's advice and beat the troll child in the hope of recovering his own. "It's probably best that he does it," she thought.

But her husband had barely struck the troll child before she rushed up and grabbed his arm. "No, don't hit him, don't hit him!" she begged.

"Then you obviously don't want to recover our child," her husband replied, struggling to free himself.

"Of course I want him back," said his wife, "but not this way."

The farmer raised his arm for another blow, but before he could strike, his wife threw herself over the child, so that the cane struck her instead.

"Good heavens!" said her husband. "Now I understand: you intend to make our child spend the rest of his life with the trolls."

He stood motionless and waited, but his wife lay there before him, protecting the troll child. The man then threw down the cane and walked out of the cottage, indignant and sorrowful.

Days of sadness and grief followed. It can be difficult enough for a mother to lose her child, but what could be worse than to have him replaced by a changeling? It holds her longing ever alive and never allows it to rest in peace.

"I don't know what I should feed the changeling," the farmer's wife told her husband one morning. "He never wants to eat what I put in front of him."

"There's nothing strange about that," said her husband. "Trolls eat frogs and mice."

"Are you saying that I should catch frogs for him?" said the farmer's wife.

"No, of course not," said her husband. "I think it would be best if he starved to death."

A whole week passed, and the farmer's wife was still unable to induce the troll infant to eat. She tempted him with delicacies of

every kind imaginable, but he spit out every choice morsel she
offered him.

One night the cat came scampering into the room with a rat in its
mouth. The farmer's wife snatched the rat away from the cat and
threw it to the changeling, then left the room in all haste to avoid see-
ing the troll child eat it.

When the farmer saw that his wife had actually begun collecting
frogs and spiders for the troll child, he felt such a loathing for her
that it was impossible for him to say a kind word to her.

And that was not all. The servants began showing disobedience and
disrespect to their lady. Their master pretended not to notice, but his
wife now realized that if she continued defending the changeling,
every day of her life would be filled with hardship and pain.

The truth was that the more she suffered for the sake of the
changeling, the more protective of him she became.

One morning the farmer's wife sat in the cottage, sewing one patch after another onto the changeling's frock. "Alas," she thought as she sewed. "It's no life strewn with roses, taking care of another's child."

She sewed and sewed, but the holes were so large and numerous that tears came to her eyes when she saw them.

"There's one thing I know," she thought. "If I were mending my own son's frock, I wouldn't be counting the holes.

"The changeling causes me nothing but agony," she continued. "Perhaps it would be best if I took him so deep into the forest that he could never find his way home again, and then left him there.

"But I really wouldn't have to go to so much trouble to be rid of him," she went on. "If I merely let him out of my sight for a moment, he would drown in the well or burn in the fireplace or be bitten by the dog or kicked by the horse. Yes, it would be an easy matter to get

rid of him, reckless and naughty as he is. Everyone on the farm despises him, and if he weren't always in my company, someone would soon find an opportunity to get him out of the way."

She walked over and gazed down at the child, who lay sleeping in a corner of the cottage. He had grown larger and become even uglier than when she first set eyes on him. His mouth had been drawn out into a snout, his eyebrows were like two stiff brushes, and his skin was like leather.

"I suppose I must keep mending your clothes and caring for you," she thought. "It's the least I can do for you. But my husband loathes me, the farm hands scorn me, the maids laugh at me, the cat hisses at the sight of me, the dog growls and shows his teeth—all because of you.

"But I could tolerate being despised," she exclaimed. "The worst of it is that every time I look at you I yearn so for my own child. Alas, my own little lambkin, where are you? Are you lying on moss and twigs, with that wicked old troll hag?"

The door opened and the farmer's wife rushed back to her sewing. Her husband walked in. He looked happy and spoke more kindly to her than he had in some time.

"There's a market over in the village today. What do you say? Shall we go?"

The suggestion made the farmer's wife happy, and she said that she would like to go.

"Get yourself ready, then, as fast as you can!" said her husband. "We must go on foot, for the horses are out to pasture. But if we take the path over the mountain, we should arrive in good time."

A few minutes later the farmer's wife stood in the doorway, happy and dressed in her Sunday best. She had totally forgotten about the troll child.

"But," she thought suddenly, "what if my husband is only trying to lure me away so that the farm hands can slay the changeling in my absence?" She walked quickly into the cottage and returned with the big troll child in her arms.

"Can't you leave that thing at home?" said her husband. Rather than sounding angry, he spoke in a soft voice.

"No, I dare not leave him," she answered.

"Well, it's your own affair," said the farmer, "but it will be a heavy load for you to carry over the mountain."

They started off on their journey, but it soon became difficult, for the path was steep. The farmer's wife grew so tired that she could hardly take another step. Time after time, she tried to persuade the troll baby to walk on his own, but he refused.

Her husband was in fine spirits and more amiable than he had been since they had lost their son. "Hand me the changeling," he said, "and let me carry him awhile."

"No, no, I can manage all right," said the farmer's wife. "I don't want to bother you with the troll brat."

"Why should you struggle with him all alone?" he said, and took the child from her.

At the very spot where the farmer took the child, the path was most difficult. It jutted out to the edge of a steep ravine and was so narrow that there was barely space for one foot at a time. All of a sudden, the farmer's wife grew frightened that something might happen to her husband while he was carrying the child.

"Walk slowly here!" she shouted, for she thought he was walking far too fast and carelessly. Shortly afterward he did stumble and came ever so close to dropping the child into the chasm.

"If the child had really fallen, we would have been rid of him for good," she thought. But in that same instant she understood that her husband had intended to throw the child down into the chasm and then pretend that it had happened by accident.

"So that was it," she thought. "He has arranged all this so he could do away with the changeling without my noticing that he did it deliberately. Well, I suppose it would be for the best if I let him do as he wishes."

Once more her husband stumbled on a stone, and once more the changeling nearly slipped from his arms. "Hand me the child! You're going to fall," said his wife.

"No," said her husband, "I'll be careful."

When he stumbled for the third time, he reached out his arms to grab hold of a tree branch, and the child fell.

His wife plunged forward, caught hold of an edge of the troll child's clothing, and pulled him up onto the path.

Her husband then turned toward her. His face was now ugly and utterly transformed. "You weren't nearly so quick when you let our child fall in the forest," he said angrily.

His wife did not answer. It had distressed her so much to learn that her husband's kindness was false that she started to cry.

"Why are you crying?" he said harshly. "It wouldn't have been such a great tragedy if I had allowed the changeling to fall. Come on, or we'll be too late."

"I don't feel like going to the market now," she said.

"You don't? Well, neither do I," he said.

As they walked home, the farmer asked himself just how much longer he could live this way. He felt that if he now made use of his strength and wrenched the child from her, he and his wife could be happy again together. He was about to start struggling with her for the child when he caught sight of her eyes, which were resting upon him, mournful and anxious. He restrained himself once more for her sake, and everything remained as it had been.

One summer night the farmstead caught on fire. By the time the servants sleeping around the hearth and in the small chamber awakened, the rooms were filled with smoke, and the attic was a great sea of flames. It was impossible even to think of extinguishing the fire or salvaging any belongings; only by rushing outside could anyone hope to avoid burning to death.

The farmer stood looking at his burning house.

"There's just one thing I'd like to know," he said, "and that is, Who has brought this misfortune upon me?"

"Why, who else could it be but the changeling?" said a farm hand. "He's been gathering sticks and straw for ages and burning them inside and out."

"Yesterday he carried a pile of dry twigs up to the attic," said a maid, "and was just about to set fire to it when I stopped him."

"If only he'd burn to death inside," said the farmer, "then I wouldn't mind that my old cottage had gone up in flames."

As he said this, his wife came out of the house, dragging the child behind her. The farmer went running up to her, grabbed the changeling, lifted him high, and flung him back into the burning house.

The farmer's wife stared at her husband for an instant, deathly pale with terror. Then she turned and rushed inside the house to fetch the child.

"And you can burn with him!" her husband shouted after her.

But she returned, and with her was the troll child. Her hands were burned, and her hair was almost singed off. No one said a word to her when she walked over to the well, smothered a few sparks that were burning on the hem of her skirt, and then sat down, with her back against the wellhouse. The troll child lay upon her lap and soon fell asleep. The woman sat erect and wide awake, staring sadly in front of her. A great number of people rushed past her, heading toward the burning house, but no one spoke to her.

At daybreak, after the house had burned to the ground, her husband walked up to her. "I can bear this no longer," he said. "You must know that it is not easy for me to leave you, but I can no longer live with that troll. I shall go my own way now, and never return."

His wife heard these words and watched him turn and walk away. She wanted to run after him, but the troll child lay heavily on her lap. She did not have the strength to shake him off, so she just sat where she was.

The farmer now headed up the mountain, telling himself that he was probably taking this path for the last time.

He had gone only a short distance when a little boy came running toward him. He was fair and as slender as a young tree. His hair was soft as silk and his eyes glistened like steel.

"Alas, that's how my own son would have looked if only he hadn't been taken from me!" said the farmer.

"Good morning!" greeted the farmer. "Where are you going?"

"And good morning to you, too!" said the child. "If you can guess who I am, then you shall know where I'm going."

When the farmer heard the child's voice, he turned quite pale.

"You speak the way my kinsmen do," he said. "And if my son weren't with the trolls, I'd say that you were he."

"You guessed correctly, Father," said the boy, laughing. "And since you guessed correctly, I shall tell you that I'm on my way to see my mother."

"Your mother? Oh no, you're not," said the farmer. "She doesn't care about you, or me. She has no heart for anyone other than a big, ugly troll child."

"Is that true, Father?" said the boy, looking his father deep in the eyes. "Then perhaps I should stay with you."

The farmer was so overjoyed at having his boy back that his eyes brimmed with tears. "Yes, you shall stay only with me!" he said, taking the boy in his arms and lifting him high up into the air. He was so frightened of losing the boy again that he walked on with the child in his arms.

When they had taken only a few steps, the boy began talking.

"You won't treat me as cruelly as you did the changeling, will you, Father?" he said.

"What do you mean?" asked the farmer.

"Well, one day the troll crone was walking on the other side of the ravine with me in her arms, and every time you stumbled and were about to drop the changeling, she was on the point of letting me fall."

"What's that you said? You were walking on the other side of the ravine?" said the farmer, anxiously.

"I'd never been so frightened," said the boy. "When you threw the troll child down into the chasm, the troll crone tried to throw me down there too. If it hadn't been for Mother . . ."

The farmer slowed his gait now and tried to grasp what the child was telling him. "You must tell me how the trolls treated you."

"I suffered at times," said the little boy, "but as long as Mother was kind to the troll child, the troll crone was kind to me."

"Did she beat you?" asked the farmer.

"She beat me no more often than you beat her child."

"Did she feed you well?" the father asked.

"When the troll child was given bread and meat, the troll crone offered me snakes and thistles. At first I almost starved to death. But when Mother gave the troll child frogs and mice, I got bread and butter. If it hadn't been for Mother . . ."

When the child said this, the farmer turned on his heels and started walking rapidly down toward the valley. "Why do you smell of smoke?" he asked.

"Well, there's nothing strange about that," said the child. "I was flung into the fire last night. If it hadn't been for Mother . . ."

The farmer was now in such a hurry that he was practically running, but suddenly he stopped. "Tell me now, why did the troll crone decide to set you free?" he said.

"When Mother sacrificed what was dearer to her than life itself, the trolls no longer had power over me, and they let me go," said the boy.

"She sacrificed something that was dearer to her than life itself?" asked the farmer.

"Yes," said the boy, "when she let you go in order to save the troll child."

The farmer's wife was still sitting beside the well. She felt as if she

had been turned to stone. She could not bring herself to move, and she saw little of what was happening around her. Then she heard her husband's voice calling her name from far away, and her heart began beating again. She opened her eyes and looked around. She saw that it was a glorious day, the sun was shining, the larks were warbling. But when she saw the charred beams that lay all around her, and the people with blackened hands and flushed faces, she knew that she had awakened to a life that was even more sorrowful than her old one. Still, she had the feeling that her suffering had finally come to an end. She looked around for the changeling. He was not on her lap, and he was nowhere to be seen.

Once more she heard her husband calling her. He came out of the forest, down the narrow path leading toward the farm, and all of the servants and neighbors who had helped fight the fire ran toward him and surrounded him, so that she was unable to see him. She could only hear how he kept calling her name.

There was great joy in his voice, but she sat there, motionless. She did not dare to move. Finally, her husband broke through the crowd of people who had gathered around him and walked up and laid a beautiful child in her arms.

"Here is our son. He has returned to us," said her husband, "and it was you, and no one else, who rescued him."

◆

Selma Lagerlöf was the first woman to win the Nobel Prize in Literature in 1909. A teacher for ten years before she started writing, Ms. Lagerlöf created nearly thirty novels for adults. Her work for children includes *The Wonderful Adventures of Nils,* which was commissioned as a geography textbook and quickly became a classic. This is the first English-language edition of *The Changeling.*

Selma Lagerlöf died in 1940.

Jeanette Winter is the author and illustrator of many books for children, including *Follow the Drinking Gourd* and, most recently, *Diego,* a collaboration with her son Jonah Winter. Another son, Max, is also a writer. The daughter of Swedish immigrants, Ms. Winter has always felt close ties to her heritage. She lives with her husband, painter Roger Winter, in rural Maine.

Susanna Stevens is a translator who divides her time between homes in Sweden and France and visits to the United States.